W9-AKU-041

Some of the Days of
Everett Anderson

Rm 9

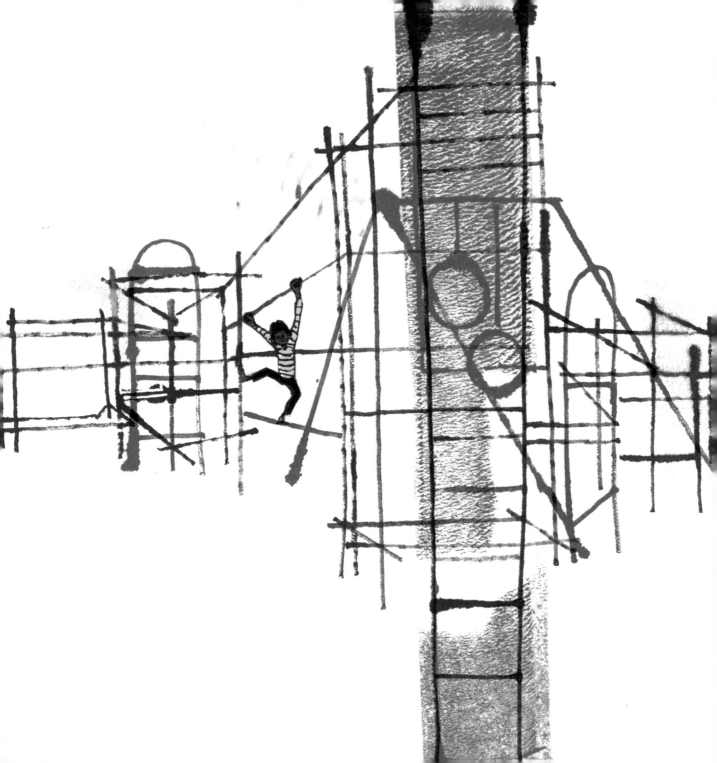

Some of the Days of Everett Anderson

BY LUCILLE CLIFTON

ILLUSTRATED BY EVALINE NESS

Henry Holt and Company · New York

Text copyright © 1970 by Lucille Clifton
Illustrations copyright © 1970 by Evaline Ness
All rights reserved, including the right to reproduce this
book or portions thereof in any form.
Published by Henry Holt and Company, Inc.,
115 West 18th Street, New York, New York 10011.
Published in Canada by Fitzhenry & Whiteside Limited,
195 Allstate Parkway, Markham, Ontario L3R 4T8.
Library of Congress Catalog Card Number: 78-98922

ISBN 0-8050-0290-1 (hardcover)
10   9   8   7   6   5   4
ISBN 0-8050-0289-8 (paperback)
10   9   8

Printed in Mexico

To my children—Sid, Rica,
Chan, Gilly, Baggy, and Neen

Monday
Morning
Good Morning

Being six
is full of tricks
and Everett Anderson knows it.

Being a boy
is full of joy
and Everett Anderson shows it.

Tuesday All Day
Rain

Everett Anderson
absolutely
refuses to lose his
umbrella.

Everett Anderson
absolutely
is pleased to leave it
at home.

Rain or shine
he doesn't whine
about "catching cold" or
"summer showers."

Sad or merry
he doesn't carry
the thing around for
hours and hours.

Everett Anderson
absolutely
would rather get wet
than to forget.

Everett Anderson
absolutely
refuses to lose his
umbrella.

Wednesday Noon Adventure

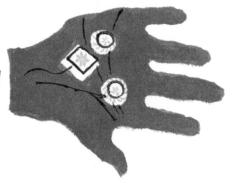

Who's black
and runs
and loves to hop?
Everett Anderson does.

Who's black
and was lost
in the candy shop?
Everett Anderson was.

Who's black
and noticed the
peppermint flowers?
Everett Anderson did.

Who's black
and was lost for
hours and hours?
Everett Anderson

                        Hid!

Thursday Evening
Bedtime

Afraid of the dark
is afraid of Mom
and Daddy
and Papa
and Cousin Tom.

"I'd be as silly
as I could be,
afraid of the dark
is afraid of Me!"

says ebony
Everett
Anderson.

Friday
Waiting for Mom

When I am seven
Mama can stay
from work and play with me
all day.

I won't go to school,
I'll pull up a seat
by her and we can talk
and eat

and we will laugh
at how it ends;
Mama and
Everett Anderson—
Friends.

Friday
Mom Is Home
Payday

Swishing one finger
in the foam
of Mama's glass
when she gets home
is a very
favorite thing to do.
Mama says
foam is a comfort,
Everett Anderson
says so too.

Saturday Night Late

The siren seems so far away
when people live in 14 A,
they can pretend that all the noise
is just some other girls and boys
running and
laughing and
having fun
instead of whatever it is
whispers
Everett Anderson.

Sunday Morning Lonely

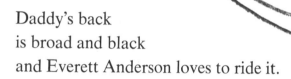

Daddy's back
is broad and black
and Everett Anderson loves to ride it.

Daddy's side
is black and wide
and Everett Anderson sits beside it.

Daddy's cheek
is black and sleek
and Everett Anderson kisses it.

Daddy's space
is a black empty place
and Everett Anderson misses it.

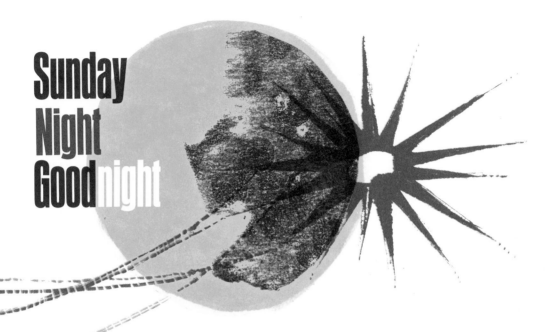

Sunday Night Goodnight

The stars are so near
to 14 A
that after playing outside
all day
Everett Anderson likes to pretend
that stars are where
apartments end.

About the Author

Lucille Clifton, poet, storyteller, college professor, mother of six and grandmother of four, is the author of many books for young readers. Seven of her picture books with Henry Holt feature Everett Anderson, including *Everett Anderson's Goodbye* (a Coretta Scott King Award winner), *Everett Anderson's Nine Month Long,* and *Everett Anderson's Christmas Coming*.

Ms. Clifton lives in Maryland.

About the Illustrator

Evaline Ness (1911–86) garnered much acclaim during her long and prolific career as a children's book illustrator. Her many books include the Caldecott Medal winner *Sam, Bangs & Moonshine*, which she also wrote, and the Caldecott Honor Books *All in the Morning Early* and *A Pocketful of Cricket*.